So Many Ways to
Live in Society

A new way to explore the animal kingdom

Editorial Director
Caroline Fortin

Research and Editing
Martine Podesto

Research and Documentation
Anne-Marie Brault

Cover Design
Épicentre

Page Setup
Lucie Mc Brearty

Illustrations
François Escalmel
Jocelyn Gardner
Rielle Lévesque
Marie-Andrée Lemieux
(Malem)

Translator
Gordon Martin

Copy Editing
Veronica Schami

QUÉBEC AMÉRIQUE

Strength in numbers!

No human being can live in complete isolation. We all rely on each other to feed, house and defend ourselves, as well as to reproduce and care for our children. All animals also have to gather together at some point in their lives. Some do so temporarily, while others remain together throughout their lives; some form simple groups, while others form highly organized societies. Living in a group has many advantages. As the saying goes, "there is strength in numbers"! Together, animals are stronger; they are better able to defend themselves, hunt, feed, raise their young and survive in the wild.

Hunting as a pack

If you intend to hunt something bigger than yourself, joining forces with others is a very good idea. Like lions and wolves, African hunting dogs form merciless hunting packs. During the day, these wild dogs roam African savannahs in groups of approximately 20. Taking turns at the head of the pack, these ravenous animals pursue and harass impalas, gazelles and wildebeests until their exhausted prey surrender.

African hunting dog
Lycaon pictus

Are you curious?

In the animal world, the strongest and most robust individuals are often the first to feed. However, among African hunting dogs, the youngest and the oldest have the privilege of eating first.

Collective incubation

Among several bird species, such as penguins, flamingos and pelicans, everyone works together to ensure that the young get all the care they need. The white-winged chough displays great solidarity in building a collective nest from bits of mud and wood. Two females in the group then lay all the eggs – about 10 or so – but the entire group watches over and sits on them until they hatch 13 to 25 days later.

white-winged chough
Corcorax melanorhamphos

chaffinch
Fringilla coelebs

All for one and one for all!

Many small birds, including sparrows, chickadees, robins, warblers and thrashers, gather together to defend themselves against the dangerous birds of prey and the owls in their area. Some of these birds, such as the chaffinch, perform an impressive aerial ballet specifically designed to intimidate intruders, who are forced to flee the dizzying barrage of pirouettes and headlong charges.

3

A community trap

Tiny Mexican spiders, barely five millimeters long, gain a considerable advantage from group living. Gathered into colonies of about 100 individuals, these little insects combine their efforts to build an immense web around the branches of a tree. This very elaborate trap, which even includes shelters and little rooms, can ensnare prey large enough to feed the entire colony at one sitting.

communal spider
Mallos gregalis

These ones enjoy the
comforts of family life

In nature, males and females have to get together to reproduce. However, after the deed is done, one parent is often left alone to bring up the little ones. But other animals find the comforts of family life most pleasant and reassuring. This group, which includes some birds, fish, reptiles and mammals, stay together to care for their young, who have to be watched over and fed until they are old enough to fend for themselves. Although some animals form new couples at the beginning of every mating season, others, such as eagles, beavers, dingoes and jackals, remain together forever.

Lifelong couples

Male and female geese and swans remain devoted to each other for their entire lives. Among whooper swans, both parents are involved in rearing the young and the birds always travel on water as a family unit. Led by their mother, the young swans sometimes climb onto her back to take comfort in her soft feathers. Meanwhile, the father watches over his offspring from the rear, warding off all danger.

4

whooper swan
Cygnus cygnus

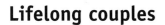

Are you curious?

Geese, ducks and swans belong to the same family. Very closely related to geese, swans are distinguished from them by their long necks, which allow them to feed in deeper water.

A joyous family

These birds, which can be heard sniggering and giggling in the wee hours of the morning, are known as kookaburras or laughing jackasses. Members of the same family as kingfishers, kookaburras form large communities whose members share the same territory. Though they are capable of reproducing, young kookaburras remain with their parents, brothers and sisters for the first few years of their adult life. They don't leave the group until it's time to start families of their own.

Australian laughing jackass
Dacelo gigas

Long live the family!

The dozen or so dwarf mongooses that choose to live in a termitarium are all brothers and sisters. For as long as their parents are alive and can still reproduce, all the offspring remain in the group, helping each other care for the newborn and keeping the entire family safe. Even young females who have never given birth can produce milk to feed their little brothers and sisters!

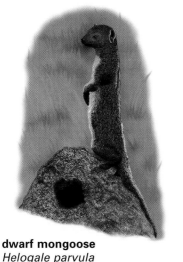

dwarf mongoose
Helogale parvula

5

Brothers and sisters together

The bat-eared fox, an African mammal with enormous ears and silvery fur, is a proud representative of the vulpine group. Bat-eared fox families are made up of a lifelong couple and their offspring of all ages, born in various litters. Young bat-eared foxes, which become adult-sized in only six months, stay with their parents to help them raise the next generation of cubs.

bat-eared fox
Otocyon megalotis

Some animals prefer to live in society
Reproductive harems

Few animals live in small family units. Most of them choose to form larger groups and live in society. United to protect themselves against predators, to find food, to care for their young and to control their territory, these animals travel as a group, recognize each other and communicate with each other. And the societies animals form are as infinitely complex as nature itself!

Some animal societies are formed primarily for reproductive purposes and consist of one male surrounded by several females; these groups are known as harems. During the mating season, the male harem leaders assemble a group of females that can produce offspring. They reserve the right to mate with these females and vigorously defend their territory against intrusions by all other males.

Societies of the African plains

Burchell's zebra, or the common zebra, forms harems made up of one male, six mares and their foals. When they are old enough to reproduce, the young females leave the group and go in search of a male who is seeking to expand his harem. As for the young males, they live in small separate groups until the day finally arrives that they can form their own "societies".

Burchell's zebra
Equus burchelli

6

The winner gets the girl

It's the beginning of spring in the Arctic. Elephant seals emerge from the icy waters of the northern seas and climb ashore, where they form harems that last for the duration of the mating season. Violent fights allow the victorious males to lay claim to the choice stretches of shoreline – and to the largest number of females! Average males attract between 10 and 20 females, but the strongest have harems of about 40 or as many as a 100!

northern elephant seal
Mirounga angustirostris

chuckwalla
Sauromalus obesus

Reproduction denied!

Most reptiles lead solitary lives. However, one large South American lizard forms what might be considered a harem. One male occupies a very large territory within which he exercises absolute power. Although subordinate males are permitted to live in the area, only the reigning tyrant can woo females during the mating season. He even goes as far as to banish the other males for the duration of this period!

Nordic harems

Group living holds no more secrets for the caribou. Fond of the safety a gregarious existence provides, this imposing beast migrates in herds of up to 50,000 individuals! When it's time to reproduce, each male caribou forms a temporary harem of 10 to 15 females. After they give birth, the new mothers leave the harem with their fawns and rejoin a group of females.

woodland caribou
Rangifer tarandus caribou

Are you
curious?

Each species of zebra has its own pattern of stripes. And each individual zebra has distinctive markings that set it apart from its fellow creatures. These differences undoubtedly help zebras recognize each other.

Some animals prefer to live in society
Groups of females

In many animals species, the females assume most of the responsibilities related to caring for the young. It is thus not surprising that many animal societies revolve around mothers who head up families. These female societies are often made up of sisters, their daughters and their daughters' offspring. These groups of sisters, aunts and cousins form matriarchal societies where co-operation and mutual support are the order of the day!

Female mountain climbers

Female Rocky Mountain goats travel in groups that include their kids. As for the males, they form separate groups or live alone, joining the females only during the reproductive season. But the females would not make them feel particularly welcome anyway. Mistresses of their domains, adult nanny goats do not hesitate to assert their authority by meting out firm blows with their horns.

Rocky Mountain goat
Oreamnos americanus

Are you curious?

During the mating season, male mountain goats dig holes in which they first urinate then roll around until they are soaked to the skin. The dirtiest, smelliest males have the best of chance of finding a mate!

ring-tailed coati
Nasua nasua

Large clans of females

This pretty little carnivore with a long turned-up nose is a member of the rat family. About the size of a cat, these animals form groups of 20 to 50 or more females and their offspring. Solitary, the males join the clan only during the reproductive period, preventing any males who are too forward from doing the same. Even males barely two years old are driven out of the group.

Marine societies

These little white whales, which are often referred to by their Russian name, beluga, form small groups of about 15 members, made up of females and their offspring. Baby belugas remain with their mothers for several years. The young females do not reach adulthood until they are about five years old. As for the young males, who do not reach maturity until about the age of eight, they eventually leave their mothers to form separate groups of males.

white whale
Delphinapterus leucas

A leader of society

The largest land animal lives in a very highly structured society made up of a core group of females accompanied by their young. Very attached to each other, these sisters, mothers and daughters help protect each other and guide the baby elephants. The group is led by its most experienced member, a female elephant who is about 50 years old. Living in isolation, the males visit the females only to reproduce.

African elephant
Loxodonta africana

Some animals prefer to live in society
Leadership hierarchies

To ensure that order and peace reign in their society, animals, like humans, have created laws. These are often based on the domination of certain individuals by others. As a general rule, adults have authority over younger animals and males dominate females. Depending on the species, it can be either the age or the size of the animals that determines superiority, but more often than not, hierarchies are established by means of fights and bloody battles. Dominant animals have numerous advantages: they not only get the best food and the largest number of female partners, they also live longer. On the other hand, they must shoulder quite a heavy burden: they have to protect their society and find food for all its members.

grey wolf
Canis lupus

Young leaders

Social rank is established very early among wolves. By fighting with each other, wolf cubs determine their place in society when still very young. A dominant couple reigns over its offspring, and several close relatives make up the rest of the herd. Larger and stronger, the dominant male generally leads the pack, organizes hunting expeditions and deals with intruders. He is followed in the hierarchy by the other males, his female partner, the other females and, lastly, the young wolves.

Pecking order

As soon as they find themselves in a group, domestic hens start defining the rules they will live by. Two by two, tirelessly, they peck away at each other. The winner of each battle takes on another winner, and so on and so on, until the champion of the tournament is declared. Each remaining hen then takes up her position in the pecking order based on the fights she has won. The hens highest up on the hierarchy have the right to express their superiority by continuing to peck away at their inferiors.

domestic hen
Gallus domesticus

Social marsupials

Whiptail wallabies are clearly the most social of marsupials. Living in groups of 30 to 50, they form communities made up of smaller temporary groups that come together to feed or simply to rest. Generally peaceful, the adult males often fight over the females. By doing so, they establish a hierarchy that determines which male can mate with the fertilized females.

whiptail wallaby
Macropus parryi

A strictly regulated society of birds

Closely related to ravens and crows, jackdaws live in groups all year long in cavities in trees, walls, ruins and steeples. Established by fights at the beginning of each season, the rules of jackdaw society are strict: no male can "marry" a female whose social rank is superior to his own, and each female automatically assumes the social rank of her "husband".

jackdaw
Corvus monedula

Are you
curious?

The expression "hungry like a wolf" reflects the eating habits of these canines. In fact, these animals can wolf down up to 10 kilos of meat per day! But they are also capable of fasting for several days in a row.

These ones don't just
monkey around

Apes are among the most skilful builders of societies. More intelligent than all other land animals, most of these inventive and curious primates organize their lives in accordance with very strict rules. As is the case among most other animals, the types of societies found among the various primate species are very dependent on the lifestyle of each species. Primates that live in the treetops have very little to fear from predators. That's why the individual members of these species travel alone or in small groups. However, baboons, macaques and chimpanzees, which live and feed on the ground, are more vulnerable to the attacks of predators. To protect themselves, they thus have to gather together and help each other. Their tribes are often made up of about 100 individuals.

ring-tailed lemur
Lemur catta

Very highly organized societies

These inhabitants of the mountains of Madagascar appreciate the advantages of group living. Grouped into troops of approximately 20 individuals, these little primates with black circles around their white tails live and raise their young together. Their groups are highly organized and are governed by strict rules: although outnumbered by the males, the adult females in the group, especially the oldest ones, are its most highly respected members.

Are you curious?

One of the favorite pastimes of the ring-tailed lemur is group sunbathing. Seated with their outstretched arms and legs reaching for the sun, they allow themselves to be caressed by the sun's hot rays. What better way to relax after a meal?

Peaceful families

Gibbons, which leap skilfully from branch to branch, form small, very tightly knit family units. The mother and father, who are devoted to each other, valiantly defend their territory by biting members of neighboring families that get too close. Since the parents can have only one baby about every two or three years and these babies do not reach adulthood until the age of seven, these small families, which include two to four offspring, remain intact for quite some time.

white-handed gibbon
Hylobates lar

Solitary apes

Orangutans live in the trees, alone. The females, accompanied by their last-born babies, spend their days searching for the fruit, leaves, pieces of bark and birds' eggs on which they feed. Solitary, the males occasionally join small groups of females, which are formed only during the mating season.

13

orangutan
Pongo pygmaeus

Small arboreal families

Barely 30 to 40 centimeters long, these arboreal primates inhabit the rainforests of South America. Their small families, which are made up of a male and a female and one or two offspring, always travel as a group. Lifelong partners, the parents occupy and aggressively defend an area approximately 50 meters in diameter. When the magic moment arrives, the two lovers lie down side by side, with their long tails tenderly intertwined.

orabussu titi
Callicebus moloch

And these monkeys mean business

All kinds of social life are found among the 181 species of primates: solitary species, couples and harems, as well as troops of males and females that share the same territory. The groups formed by primates tend to be very stable and the bonds between the various individuals are extremely strong and important. They rely on numerous means of communication: cries, grooming sessions, caresses and facial expressions carry messages as clear as those conveyed by human languages.

A wise animal with a silvery back

The gorilla is the largest living primate and undoubtedly one of the most intelligent land animals. The giant of the African forests, it lives in small harems, generally made up of five to 10 individuals, where a single adult male watches over a number of females and their young. This mild-mannered, attentive and protective patriarch – known as "silver back" due to the white hairs in the fur on its back – is solely responsible for the cohesion of the entire group.

14

gorilla
Gorilla gorilla

Community life

Common chimpanzees live in communities made up of as many as 100 males and females. Within these communities, various smaller groups can be formed. Some of these include mothers and their newborns, while others are made up of males who defend the limits of the community's territory. Among chimpanzees, males dominate females and older females dominate younger females.

common chimpanzee
Pan troglodytes

Harems headed by women

Red guenons – which are also known as patas, Hussar, military or dancing red monkeys – roam the African plains in small groups of six to 30 individuals. Although they live in harems, the females occupy the dominant position in the red guenon hierarchy. One of them, the dominant female, leads the troop, and the females prevail when conflicts arise. The males are responsible only for protecting the group.

red guenon
Erythrocebus patas

Subjugated females

Among hamadryas baboons, the smallest family unit is a harem made up of an extremely jealous and possessive male and the five to 10 females who must remain at his beck and call – or else… Several harems often unite to form clans of 10 to 20 baboons. Together, these hamadryas clans form troops of approximately 70 animals.

hamadryas baboon
Papio hamadryas

Are you curious?

There are only a few thousand gorillas left in the wild, and this number continues to decline dramatically. African deforestation and hunting are the main threats to the survival of these animals.

Among these ones, everyone
has a role to play

Some animals have achieved absolute perfection when it comes to social organization. Among these species, the work done by each and every member is regulated and structured to such an extent that no individual could survive on his or her own! For example, every aspect of the lives of social insects is strictly organized and each individual in the colony is assigned a specific role at birth. Individuals that inherit the same role – kings, queens, soldiers, workers and drones – look identical and are divided into groups known as "castes". No matter what their role, all members of the colony tirelessly perform a colossal number of tasks to ensure the survival of the group as a whole.

A queen's life

Of the 50,000 to 80,000 bees living under the same roof, just one female – the queen – is responsible for reproduction. About 100 males, the drones, are entrusted with the task of mating with the queen, while tens of thousands of sterile worker bees take care of everything else: they build, clean and repair the cells, watch over and feed the larvae, and gather the nectar then store it the cells of the hive.

honeybee
Apis mellifera

An insect society made up of mammals

These rodents with pink, bare, wrinkled skin live in colonies of about 40 individuals that are divided into castes, just like the colonies of social insects! The queen is surrounded by little individual males and females: these are the workers, who are responsible for building an impressive network of tunnels and for finding food. Meanwhile, the large soldiers, the defence force, spend most of their time snoozing.

naked mole rat
Heterocephalus glaber

A termite monarchy

Two million species of termites inhabit the earth, forming colonies of up to a million individuals! Each colony revolves around a couple, the king and queen, who are the only ones permitted to reproduce. Once fertilized, the queen becomes enormous and can no longer move. While the big-jawed soldiers defend the colony, the workers provide food for all the inhabitants and construct and maintain the termitarium.

termite
isoptera order

The birth of an ant hill

Whether made up of a half dozen or several million individuals, ant societies are invariably divided into three castes: one or more queens, the males and the workers. Every so often, one queen and one male leave their native colony to found their own society. The couple then produces workers to care for the future generations and to clean and defend the ant hill. The male dies shortly after he fulfils his reproductive role.

African stink ant
Paltothyreus tarsatus

Are you curious?

The queen bee is a veritable baby factory. She lays 1,500 to 2,000 eggs per day. Given that she can survive for approximately four to five years, she has the potential to lay upwards of two million eggs over the course of her lifetime!

These ones mingle
with the crowd

Just because these animals live in groups does not mean they form societies! Incapable of recognizing each other and in some cases completely oblivious to each other, some animals nevertheless prefer the advantages of group living. Impelled by the conditions in their environment (sometimes simply attracted by a source of light or food) or by the need for protection, they cluster together in groups of mind-boggling proportions. This explains why herds of mammals, flocks of birds, swarms of insects and schools of fish migrate, hibernate, sleep, rest, reproduce or just move around in vast numbers.

Sunbathing iguanas

marine iguana
Amblyrhynchus cristatus

The Galapagos Islands offer a stunning sight: thousands of marine iguanas stretched out on the rocks in the caressing rays of the sun, warming up after a long chilly night. The one-meter-long individuals comprising these herds of reptiles go down to sea only to feed, immediately returning to their restful perches on the rocks.

18

Black clouds of locusts

Desert locusts can gather together to form swarms of several million insects. Travelling thousands of kilometers in search of food, these black clouds of ravenous locusts consume hundreds of kilos of vegetation on a daily basis, leaving ravaged landscapes in their wake.

desert locust
Schistocerca gregaria

Everyone all in a row

Moving around in Indian file – that's the trick processionary caterpillars rely on to make them feel safer. Spending the vast majority of their time together, pine processionary caterpillars – which, as their name suggests, are usually found in forests dominated by pine trees – travel in groups of up to 300, forming a train 10 meters long. Each caterpillar follows the tuft of hair emerging from the hindquarters of the preceding one.

pine processionary caterpillar
Thaumetopoe apityocampa

Mass migrations

In the right weather conditions and with the appropriate food, Norway lemmings can be extraordinarily prolific. The females, which can reproduce at the age of three weeks, give birth to as many as eight young at a time, and do so several times a year! When their territory becomes too small, these little rodents form crowds that flock toward fertile valleys in search of new spaces to live and feed.

Norway lemming
Lemmus lemmus

Are you curious?

A member of the iguana family, the marine iguana is the only marine lizard. When the tide reaches its low point, every three to five days, this lizard dives for the seaweed on which it feeds. It can dive to depths of up to 15 meters!

Some animals are
inseparable

Certain animals belong to very different species that form very close bonds based on partnership and co-operation. These "associates", who unite permanently or occasionally, tend to benefit greatly from these relationships, some of which ensure their very survival. There are three main types of partnerships. The term "commensalism" describes a relationship from which an animal benefits without inconveniencing the other partner. "Parasitism" refers to a relationship in which one animal exploits another, and "mutualism" refers to a relationship that is advantageous for both animals involved.

Comforting arms

The superb creatures known as sea anemones conceal a powerful weapon: their tentacles, which are equipped with stinging cells that can paralyze and kill any prey that ventures near. But far from being inconvenienced by these tentacles, the little clown fish found on coral reefs spend most of their time in and around the stinging cells and even raise their offspring there! The skin of clown fish is covered with protective mucus that allows them to take refuge in the arms of an anemone whenever they please.

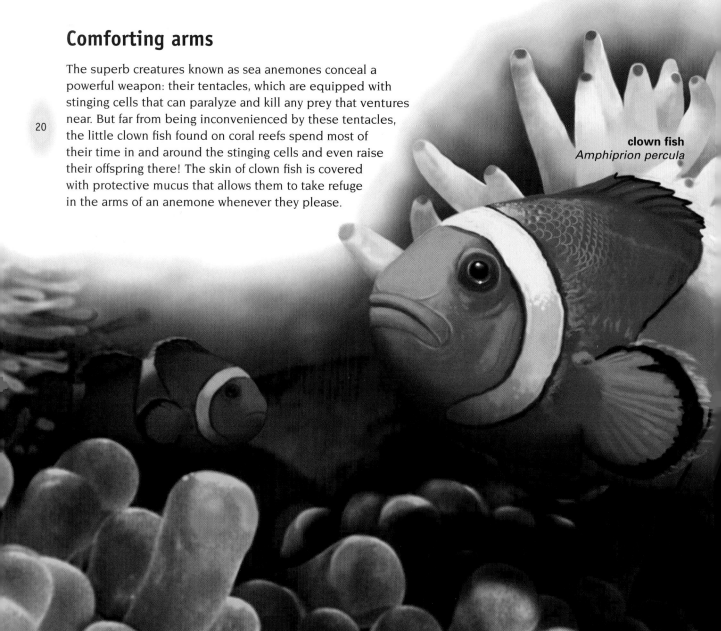

clown fish
Amphiprion percula

A safe, fast and practical means of transportation

The remora, a tropical fish, travels without expending too much energy. Instead of a main dorsal fin, it has a sucker-like organ that allows it to attach itself to the belly of a shark. Once stuck to its host in this way, the remora can traverse many miles, benefit from the protection of the shark, feed on its parasites and gather its food waste.

striped remora
Echeneis naucrates

The transportation of filters

Barnacles, which feed by filtering out the microscopic animals suspended in water, are so plentiful along coasts that they number in the hundreds of millions per square meter. These little crustaceans, which often attach themselves to rocks or boats, are particularly fond of travelling on the backs of turtles, snakes, fish and marine mammals. By covering great distances, barnacles can find a more abundant food supply.

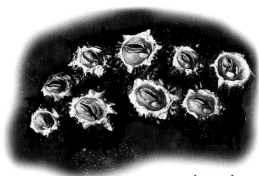

barnacle
Cryptolepas rhachianectes

21

An undesirable partner

Ticks make life hard for many poor mammals. After travelling through the fur and reaching the skin of their victim, these mites pierce the epidermis. Then, using special oral fittings, they firmly attach themselves and suck the blood of their host for several hours or even several days. Ticks sometimes carry serious diseases such as relapsing fever, cerebrospinal meningitis and tularaemia.

tick
Ixodes ricinus

Are you curious?

The anemone benefits in several ways from its relationship with the clown fish, because in addition to removing the refuse that collects on the tentacles of the anemone, the clown fish attacks potential enemies and attracts other small fish on which the anemone can feast.

But no more than
these ones

Inseparable animals are not always stuck directly to each other. They often have their very own living space, where each of them can come and go as they please. But certain associations are so beneficial that where one partner is found, the other is rarely far behind.

ratel
Mellivora capensis

United in sinful pleasure

One has a weakness for honey, and the other is a fool for beeswax. It's a match made in heaven! When a greater honeyguide spots a beehive, it attracts a ratel by crying out persistently and putting on a display that sends a clear message. Once it arrives on the scene, the ratel savours the delicious honey while its partner patiently waits to delight in the remaining honey and wax.

22

Are you curious?

The skin of the ratel is so thick that it makes the animal completely invulnerable to bee stings and even to the bites of poisonous snakes like cobras.

A good neighborhood

These little South American birds make a wise choice when it comes to the location of their colony. Pressed up against each other, their little purse-shaped nests are built in large trees overhanging streams and are often found near wasp nests. This choice location provides the birds with a measure of protection and in no way harms the wasps.

yellow-rumped cacique
Cacicus cela

common wood ant
Formica rufa

One good turn...

Although they feed on animal prey, tree sap, mushrooms and seeds, the wood ants found in coniferous forests love the sweet liquid secreted by the large blue caterpillar. Imprisoned in the ant hill, the larva of the large blue is licked greedily. But in return, it gets to feed on the ant brood in winter. Once its transformation is complete, the caterpillar emerges from the ant hill as a full-fledged butterfly.

large blue caterpillar
Maculinea arien

23

A murderous fly

Several harmless-looking flies can sometimes carry extremely serious diseases. By sucking the blood of certain wild mammals, the sleeping-sickness fly ingests dangerous microbes that it can then transmit to domestic animals or human beings. In humans, sleeping sickness is a very serious illness that causes sore throat, fever, mental disorders and even death.

tsetse fly
Glossina morsitans

greater honeyguide
Indicator indicator

While others prefer solitude

Whether they form solid couples, societies, herds, swarms or crowds, animals generally appear to be drawn to each other. However, some animals prefer to lead solitary lives. Among these animals, the only contact with other members of their species occurs during brief reproductive encounters between males and females. As soon as the deed is done, the two parents separate and either the female or male partner raises the young alone. When not fulfilling their reproductive obligations, the animals isolate themselves in an area they aggressively defend against intruders.

Solitary savannah strollers

The black rhinoceros, also known as the hook-lipped rhinoceros, is a large solitary animal that has little use for its fellow creatures. During the mating season, it has to display extraordinary patience to cajole its future partners. The parents remain together for just a few days, then separate and return to their respective territories.

black rhinoceros
Diceros bicornis

A merciless loner

This small triangular head with two large compound eyes goes practically unnoticed in grasses and foliage. Immobile, this formidable hunter stalks its prey and does not like to be disturbed, no matter what the circumstances. It guards its privacy so jealously that it doesn't hesitate to eat other mantises that enter its living space – even if the intruder in question is its mate!

European mantis
Mantis religios

polar bear
Ursus maritimus

Solitary arctic traveller

Quite intolerant of other members of its species, the male polar bear gains the right to mate by engaging in numerous fights with his rivals. The victor, generally the bigger and stronger bear, wins the heart of the female for only a very short time. In fact, once his job is done, the male bear abandons his mate, who must care for the cubs and keep the family together on her own.

Mother and "child"

This strangle little member of the giraffe family is another great loner of the virgin forests of central Africa. Well camouflaged by its streaks and brown fur, the female okapi and its most recent baby get together with a male only when it's time to mate again. These solitary animals rely on their highly developed sense of smell to locate each other.

okapi
Okapia johnstoni

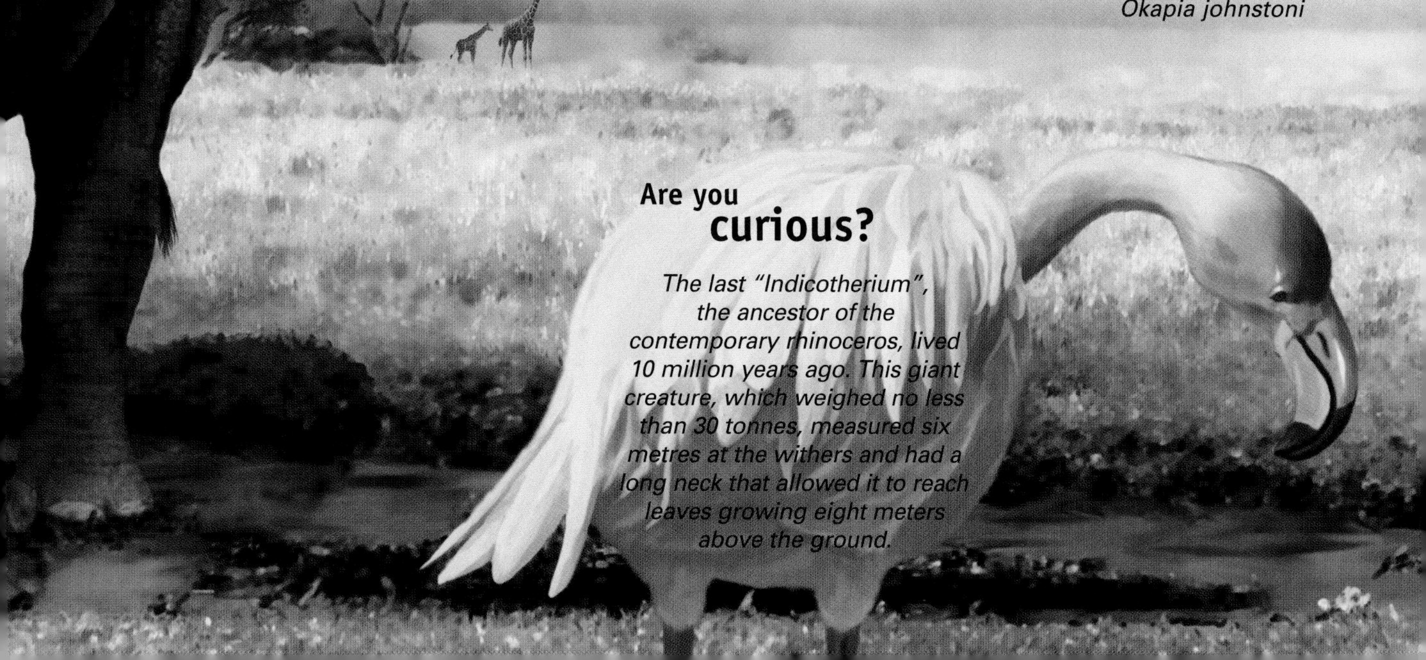

Are you curious?

The last "Indicotherium", the ancestor of the contemporary rhinoceros, lived 10 million years ago. This giant creature, which weighed no less than 30 tonnes, measured six metres at the withers and had a long neck that allowed it to reach leaves growing eight meters above the ground.

1. **African hunting dog (p. 2)**
   (Africa, south of the Sahara)

2. **White-winged chough (p. 3)**
   (Australia)

3. **Chaffinch (p. 3)**
   (Europe, western Siberia, central Asia and North Africa)

4. **Communal spider (p. 3)**
   (Mexico)

5. **Whooper swan (p. 4)**
   (nests in the Arctic, Iceland, Scandinavia and Siberia; winters in western Europe)

6. **Australian laughing jackass (p. 5)**
   (Australia, Tasmania and New Guinea)

7. **Dwarf mongoose (p. 5)**
   (Africa, south of the Sahara)

8. **Bat-eared fox (p. 5)**
   (eastern Africa, southern Ethiopia and South Africa)

9. **Burchell's zebra (p. 6)**
   (Africa: southern Ethiopia and Sudan, central Africa and eastern South Africa)

10. **Northern elephant seal (p. 7)**
    (eastern coast of the North Pacific)

11. **Chuckwalla (p. 7)**
    (southwestern United States)

12. **Woodland caribou (p. 7)**
    (eastern and western Canada)

13. **Rocky Mountain goat (p. 8)**
    (western Canada and northwestern United States)

14. **Ring-tailed coati (p. 9)**
    (South America: eastern coastal plains as far as Argentina, and as far as Ecuador in the west)

15. **White whale (p. 9)**
    (icy coasts of the Arctic Ocean and surrounding areas)

16. **African elephant (p. 9)**
    (Africa, south of the Sahara)

17. **Grey wolf (p. 10)**
    (northern North America, Asia, Middle East, Europe)

18. **Domestic hen (p. 11)**
    (raised throughout the world)

19. **Whiptail wallaby (p. 11)**
    (Australia: east of Queensland and in northeastern New South Wales)

20. **Jackdaw (p. 11)**
    (all over the world, except North America)

21. **Ring-tailed lemur (p. 12)**
    (Madagascar)

22. **White-handed gibbon (p. 13)**
    (Thailand, Malay Peninsula, northern Sumatra)

23. **Orangutan (p. 13)**
    (northern Sumatra and the plains of Borneo)

24. **Orabussu titi (p. 13)**
    (central South America: Bolivia, Brazil and Colombia)

25. **Gorilla (p. 14)**
    (West Africa and central Africa)

26. **Common chimpanzee (p. 15)**
    (western and central Africa: north of the Zaire River, from Senegal to Tanzania)

27. **Red guenon (p. 15)**
    (from western Africa to the Sudan, and in Uganda and northwestern Kenya)

28. **Hamadryas baboon (p. 15)**
    (Ethiopia, Somalia, Saudi Arabia and South Yemen)

29. **Honeybee (p. 16)**
    (originated in Asia; introduced into many countries)

30. **Naked mole rat (p. 17)**
    (eastern Africa)

31. **Termite (p. 17)**
    (North America, Asia, Europe, Australia, Africa, South America)

32. **African stink ant (p. 17)**
    (Africa)

33. **Marine iguana (p. 18)**
    (Galapagos Islands)

34. **Desert locust (p. 19)**
    (Sahel, Sahara, Arabian Peninsula and as far east as India)

35. **Pine processionary caterpillar (p. 19)**
    (southern Europe)

36. **Norway lemming (p. 19)**
    (Scandinavian tundra and northwestern Russia)

37. **Clown fish (p. 20)**
    (western and central Pacific Ocean)

38. **Striped remora (p. 21)**
    (tropical seas)

39. **Barnacle (p. 21)**
    (North Pacific)

40. **Tick (p. 21)**
    (northern Europe)

41. **Ratel and greater honeyguide (p. 22-23)**
    (Africa, from Senegal and the Sudan as far as the Cape; Asia, from Arabia to Turkistan and as far east as India)

42. **Yellow-rumped cacique (p. 23)**
    (Central and South America)

43. **Common wood ant (p. 23)**
    (Europe, Caucasia, Siberia and North America)

44. **Large blue caterpillar (p. 23)**
    (throughout Europe)

45. **Tsetse fly (p. 23)**
    (Africa)

46. **Black rhinoceros (p. 24)**
    (Africa, south of the Sahara)

47. **European mantis (p. 25)**
    (Europe, Asia, Africa, Australia and North America)

48. **Polar bear (p. 25)**
    (polar regions of the northern hemisphere, especially north of the Arctic Circle: Alaska, Canada, Greenland, Svalbard, Siberia and the Arctic Ocean)

49. **Okapi (p. 25)**
    (central Africa)

More clues for
the most curious

BRIEF GLOSSARY OF ANIMAL GROUPS		
Name of Group	**Definition**	**Examples**
Herd	A group of wild or domestic animals of the same species	Wild horses, buffalo, deer, boars, cattle, sheep
Flock	A group of wild or domestic animals of the same species	Sheep, goats, seagulls
Harem	A group of several females gathered around a male for the purpose of reproduction. The harem is fiercely defended by the male	Musk-ox, sea lion, hippopotamus
Pack	A group of animals that live together, especially predators and hunting animals	Coyotes, wolves, African hunting dogs, hounds
School of fish	A large number of fish of the same species	Herring, cod, tuna
Cloud	A large number of insects or other small animals in flight	Birds, mosquitos
Swarm	A large mass of small animals, especially insects	Bees, migrating locusts
Rookery	A colony of gregarious birds or mammals such as seals or penguins	Sea lion, emperor penguin
Colony	A group of animals that live together. This word is often used to refer to a group of birds that gather together to reproduce or to designate a group of stationary animals such as coral	Gannet, bees, coral
Troop, band	A herd or flock	Monkeys
Community	All the animal populations comprising a given ecosystem	Lacustrine community (all the fish, amphibians, birds and mammals inhabiting a particular lake)
Society	A group of individuals of the same species that move together, recognize each other, communicate with each other other and obey common rules	Wolves, elephants, most primates
Mass	A large gathering of animals without social organization	Insects around a light source, migrating butterflies

HOW MANY ARE THERE?		
	Animal	**Number**
Loners	Dragonfly *(Odonata)*	1
	Snake *(Colubridae family)*	1
	Turtle *(Chelonia)*	1
	Marten *(Mustelidae family)*	1
	Leopard *(Panthera pardus)*	1
Families	Gibbons *(Pongidae)*	3 to 4
	Swans *(Anatidae family)*	4 to 9
	Beavers *(Castoridae family)*	5 to 12
Groups	Hippopotamus *(Hippopotamus amphibius)*	10 to 15
	Blue hare *(Lepus timidus)*	15 to 30
	Japanese macaques *(Macaca fuscata)*	30 to 40
	Capybaras *(Hydrochaeris hydrochaeris)*	65
	Hyenas *(Hyaenidae family)*	100
Multitudes	Ants *(Formicidae family)*	10,000 to 100,000
	Honeybees *(Apis mellifera)*	50,000 to 80,000
	Red-billed quelea (birds) *(Quelea quelea)*	10 to 30 million
	Monarch butterflies *(Danaus plexippus)*	16 million
	Free-tailed bats *(Molossidae family)*	20 million
	Black-tailed prairie dogs *(Cynomys ludovicianus)*	400 million
	Desert locusts *(Schistocerca gregaria)*	250 billion
	Rocky Mountain locusts *(Melanoplus mexicanus)*	12,500 billion

For further information...

African hunting dog
Lycaon pictus

class	Mammalia
order	Carnivora
family	Canidae

size and weight	1.36 m, including the tail; 60 cm at the withers; 16 to 27 kg
distribution	Africa, south of the Sahara
habitat	savannahs, plains, semi-arid regions
diet	gazelles, impalas, zebras, gnus, antelopes
reproduction	2 to 12 offspring per litter; 9- to 11-week gestation period
life span	10 to 15 years

whooper swan
Cygnus cygnus

class	Birds
order	Anseriformes
family	Anatidae

size and weight	1.5 m long; 2-m wingspan; approximately 11 kg
distribution	Arctic, Iceland, Scandinavia, Siberia and north-western Europe
habitat	fresh water, marshes, lakes or bays
diet	aquatic plants, worms, molluscs and insects
reproduction	from 5 to 7 eggs, in May; 35- to 42-day incubation period
life span	up to 30 years

Burchell's zebra
Equus burchelli

class	Mammalia
order	Perissodactyla
family	Equidae

size and weight	2.1 to 2.6 m long, 300 kg
distribution	Africa, southern Europe and the Sudan, Angola, eastern South Africa
habitat	plains, savannahs, forests and scrubland
diet	grasses, leaves, bark, fruit and roots
reproduction	one foal; 330- to 375-day gestation period
predators	large carnivores

Rocky Mountain goat
Oreamnos americanus

class	Mammalia
order	Artiodactyla
family	Bovidae

size	91 cm to 1.07 m at the withers
distribution	western Canada and the north-western United States
habitat	steep escarpments and alpine meadows
diet	grasses, shrubs, flowers, coniferous buds, moss and lichen
reproduction	one kid; 178-day gestation period
predators	cougar, eagle, brown bear, wolverine, wolf, coyote

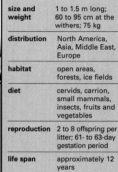

grey wolf
Canis lupus

class	Mammalia
order	Carnivora
family	Canidae

size and weight	1 to 1.5 m long; 60 to 95 cm at the withers; 75 kg
distribution	North America, Asia, Middle East, Europe
habitat	open areas, forests, ice fields
diet	cervids, carrion, small mammals, insects, fruits and vegetables
reproduction	2 to 8 offspring per litter; 61- to 63-day gestation period
life span	approximately 12 years

ring-tailed lemur
Lemur catta

class	Mammalia
order	Primata
family	Lemuridae

size and weight	between 39 and 46 cm, including the head; tail: 56 to 63 cm; 2.3 to 3 kg
distribution	Madagascar
habitat	forests and open, dry areas
diet	leaves, fruit and seeds
reproduction	one offspring per litter; 136-day gestation period
predators	birds of prey
life span	15 to 18 years in captivity

gorilla
Gorilla gorilla

class	Mammalia
order	Primata
family	Pongidae

size and weight	from 1.5 to 1.8 m tall; 90 to 180 kg
distribution	central and western Africa
habitat	secondary tropical forests
diet	plants, bushes, vines
reproduction	one baby gorilla per litter; 250- to 270-day gestation period
predators	man
life span	35 years in the wild

honeybee
Apis mellifera

class	Insecta
order	Hymenoptera
family	Apoidea

size	queen: 22 mm; drone: 19 mm; worker: 16 mm
distribution	throughout the world
habitat	open areas with an abundance of flowers
diet	nectar and pollen
reproduction	1,500 to 2,000 eggs per day
predators	birds, wasps, dragonflies
life span	queen: 5 years; drones and workers: 1 month

marine iguana
Amblyrhynchus cristatus

class	Reptilia
order	Squamata
family	Iguanidae

size and weight	up to 1.75 m long; 3.4 kg
distribution	Galapagos Islands
habitat	coasts
diet	seaweed and kelp
reproduction	2 eggs; 4-month incubation period
predators	wild dogs

clown fish
Amphiprion percula

class	Fish
order	Percomorphi
family	Pomacentridae

size	11 cm
distribution	western and central Pacific Ocean
habitat	coral reefs
diet	microscopic plants and animals
reproduction	20,000 to 25,000 eggs at a time
predators	fish
life span	over 5 years

ratel
Mellivora capensis

class	Mammalia
order	Carnivora
family	Mustelidae

size and weight	80 to 90 cm, including the tail; approximately 11 kg
distribution	Africa, Arabia, central Asia and India
habitat	rock hills, forests, savannahs or semi-arid plateaux
diet	fruit, rodents, birds and insects
reproduction	2 young per litter, 6-month gestation period
predators	large carnivores
life span	up to 20 years

black rhinoceros
Diceros bicornis

class	Mammalia
order	Perissodactyla
family	Rhinocerotidae

size and weight	from 3 to 3.75 metres; 1.4 to 1.5 m at the withers; from 1to 1.8 tonnes
distribution	Africa, south of the Sahara
habitat	wooded savannahs
diet	plants, especially acacia branches
reproduction	one calf per litter; 460-day gestation period
predators	lions (hunt the calves)
life span	40 to 50 years

Glossary

Arboreal

Living in or among trees.

Brood

Batch of eggs or larvae produced by animals such as bees.

Cohesion

Bond or force uniting the members of a group.

Compound eye

Eye made up of numerous facets, like that of a fly.

Conspecific

Individual of the same species.

Domination

Action of an individual who holds sway over others and exercises authority over them by imposing his or her choices and decisions.

Family unit

Group of individuals forming a family.

Fawn

Young of the deer or of a related species.

Fertile

Capable of producing offspring.

Generation

Set of beings born at approximately the same time and that are thus about the same age.

Gregarious

Living together in herds or in flocks.

Hierarchy

Order according to which a group is organized and within which each individual occupies a particular position.

Mammal

Animal species in which the female has mammary glands for feeding her young.

Mandible

Mouthpart in insects and crustaceans, usually one of pair, used to grasp and crush food.

Marsupial

Animal species in which the female has a ventral pouch containing mammary glands where the new-borns are carried and suckled.

Matriarchal

Where females prevail and wield the decision-making power.

Maturity

Age or period of life when an animal completes its development and becomes an adult.

Mental

Having to do with the mind or intellectual activity.

Migration

Mass movement of a single species at specific time of the year and in a specific direction.

Mucus

Transparent, viscous liquid.

Offspring

Child, young animal.

Oral

Of the mouth.

Patriarch

Older male leading a peaceful life in the bosom of his family.

Pattern

Model or shape used to reproduce a design.

Pirouette

Spinning movement designed to intimidate an intruder.

Predator

Animal that feeds on prey.

Primates

Mammals, such as apes, with a full set of teeth and hands that can grasp objects.

Progeny

Descendants of a person or animal.

Prolific

Reproducing quickly and in abundance.

Reptile

Crawling animal with scale-covered skin, such as the snake, the iguana and the tortoise.

Rodent

Mammal with sharp incisors that eats by gnawing, such as the mouse.

Social rank

Position occupied by an individual in a group in relation to the other members.

Sterile

Incapable of reproducing, having offspring.

Stinging cell

Cell that discharges an arrow-like barb and a toxin that stuns prey.

Store

To set aside for future use.

Streak

Striped marking on fur.

Subordinate

Occupying a lower rank in the social organization.

Tentacle

Elongated flexible arm, often lined with suckers, used by certain molluscs to touch and grasp.

Territory

Area an animal reserves for itself, forbidding access to others.

Withers

The highest part of the back of a quadruped.

Index

Birds

Australian laughing jackass 5
chaffinch 3
chickadees 3
domestic hen 11
ducks 4
eagles 4
emperor penguin 28
flamingos 3
gannet 28
geese 4
greater honeyguide 22, 23
jackdaw 11
kookaburras (see Laughing
jackasses) 5
laughing jackasses 5
pelicans 3
penguins 3
red-billed quelea 29
robins 3
sparrows 3
swans 4, 29
thrashers 3
warblers 3
white-winged chough 3
whooper swan 4, 30
yellow-rumped cacique 23

Fishes

clown fish 20, 21, 30
cod 28
herring 28
striped remora 21
tuna 28

Insects and other invertebrates

African stink ant 17
ants 29
barnacle 21
bees 28
common wood ant 23
communal spider 3
coral 28
desert locusts 19, 29
dragonfly 29
European mantis 25
honeybees 16, 29, 30
large blue caterpillar 23
migrating butterflies 28
migrating locusts 28
monarch butterflies 29
mosquitos 28
**pine processionary
caterpillar** 19
Rocky Mountain locusts 29
sea anemones 20
sleeping-sickness fly (see
tsetse fly) 23
termite 17
ticks 21
tsetse fly 23

Mammals

African elephant 9
African hunting dogs 2, 28, 30
apes 12
baboons 12
bat-eared fox 5
beavers 4, 29
black rhinoceros 24, 30
black-tailed prairie dogs 29
blue hare 29

boars 28
buffalo 28
burchell's zebra 6, 30
capybaras 29
cattle 28
chimpanzees 12
common chimpanzee 15
coyotes 28
deer 28
dingoes 4
dwarf mongoose 5
elephants 28
free-tailed bats 29
gibbons 29
goats 28
gorillas 14, 15, 30
grey wolf 10, 30
hamadryas baboon 15
hippopotamus 28, 29
hook-lipped rhinoceros (see
black rhinoceros) 24
hounds 28
hyenas 29
indicotherium 25
jackals 4
Japanese macaques 29
leopard 29
lions 2
macaques 12
marten 29
monkeys 28
musk-ox 28
naked mole rat 17
northern elephant seal 7
Norway lemming 19
okapi 25
orabussu titi 13
orangutan 13
patas (see red guenon) 15
polar bear 25
ratel 22, 30
red guenon 15
ring-tailed coati 9
ring-tailed lemur 12, 30
Rocky Mountain goat 8, 30
sea lion 28
seagulls 28
sheep 28
whiptail wallaby 11
white whale 9
white-handed gibbon 13
wild horses 28
wolves 2, 11, 28
woodland caribou 7
zebra 7

Reptiles

chuckwalla 7
marine iguana 18, 19, 30
snake 29
turtle 29

A

African elephant 9
African hunting dogs 2, 28, 30
African stink ant 17
amphibians 28
ants 29
apes 12
associations 20, 22
Australian laughing jackass 5

B

baboons 12
barnacle 21

bat-eared fox 5
beavers 4, 29
bees 28
birds 4, 28
black rhinoceros 24, 30
black-tailed prairie dogs 29
blue hare 29
boars 28
buffalo 28
burchell's zebra 6, 30

C

capybaras 29
castes 16, 17
cattle 28
chaffinch 3
chickadees 3
chimpanzees 12
chuckwalla 7
clown fish 20, 21, 30
cod 28
collective nest 3
colonies 3, 16, 17, 23, 28
commensalism 20
common chimpanzee 15
common wood ant 23
communal spider 3
communauty web 3
communication 14
coral 28
couples 4, 5, 14, 17
coyotes 28
crowds 18, 19

D

deer 28
desert locusts 19, 29
dingoes 4
domestic hen 11
dominant animals 10, 15
domination 10
dragonfly 29
drones 16
ducks 4
dwarf mongoose 5

E

eagles 4
elephants 28
emperor penguin 28
European mantis 25

F

families 4, 5, 13
fights 7, 10, 11
fish 4, 28
flamingos 3
flocks 18, 28
free-tailed bats 29

G

gannet 28
geese 4
gibbons 29
goats 28
gorillas 14, 15, 30
greater honeyguide 22, 23
grey wolf 10, 30

H

hamadryas baboon 15
harems 6, 7, 14, 15, 28
herds 7, 10, 18, 28
herring 28
hierarchy 10, 11
hippopotamus 28, 29
honeybees 16, 29, 30
hook-lipped rhinoceros (see
black rhinoceros) 24
hounds 28
hyenas 29

I

indicotherium 25
insects 28

J

jackals 4
jackdaw 11
Japanese macaques 29

K

kings 16, 17
kookaburras (see Laughing
jackasses) 5

L

large blue caterpillar 23
laughing jackasses 5
leopard 29
lions 2

M

macaques 12
mammals 4, 28
marine iguana 18, 19, 30
marten 29
mass 28
matriarchal societies 8, 9
migrating butterflies 28
migrating locusts 28
monarch butterflies 29
monkeys 28
mosquitos 28
musk-ox 28
mutualism 20

N

naked mole rat 17
northern elephant seal 7
Norway lemming 19

O

okapi 25
orabussu titi 13
orangutan 13

P

pack 28
parasitism 20
patas (see red guenon) 15
pelicans 3
penguins 3

**pine processionary
caterpillar** 19
polar bear 25
primates 12, 14, 28

Q

queens 16, 17

R

ratel 22, 30
red guenon 15
red-billed quelea 29
reptiles 4, 7
ring-tailed coati 9
ring-tailed lemur 12, 30
robins 3
Rocky Mountain goat 8, 30
Rocky Mountain locusts 29
rookery 28

S

schools 18
school of fish 28
sea anemones 20, 21
sea lion 28
seagulls 28
sheep 28
sleeping-sickness fly (see
tsetse fly) 23
snake 29
social rank 10
societies 6, 8, 9, 10, 11, 12, 17,
28
soldiers 16, 17
solitary 7, 8, 9, 14, 24
sparrows 3
striped remora 21
swans 4, 29
swarms 18, 19

T

termite 17
thrashers 3
ticks 21
troop 28
tsetse fly 23
tuna 28
turtle 29

W

warblers 3
whiptail wallaby 11
white whale 9
white-handed gibbon 13
white-winged chough 3
whooper swan 4, 30
wild horses 28
wolves 2, 11, 28
workers 16, 17

Y

yellow-rumped cacique 23

Z

zebra 7

The terms in **bold characters** refer to an illustration; those in *italics* indicate a keyword.

So Many Ways to Live in Society was created and produced by **QA International**, a division of
Les Éditions Québec Amérique inc, 329, rue de la Commune Ouest, 3ᵉ étage, Montréal (Québec) H2Y 2E1 Canada **T** 514.499.3000 **F** 514.499.3010
©1998 Éditions Québec Amérique inc.

ISBN 2-89037-971-X

Printed and bound in Canada

10 9 8 7 6 5 4 3 2 1   99 98